MORE MYSTERY BY KRISTINE KATHRYN RUSCH

THE RETRIEVAL ARTIST SERIES

The Disappeared

Extremes

Consequences

Buried Deep

Paloma

Recovery Man

The Recovery Man's Bargain

Duplicate Effort

The Possession of Paavo Deshin

Anniversary Day

Blowback

A Murder of Clones

Search & Recovery

The Peyti Crisis

Vigilantes

Starbase Human

Masterminds

The Impossibles

The Retrieval Artist

THE SMOKEY DALTON SERIES

WRITING AS KRIS NELSCOTT

A Dangerous Road

Smoke-Filled Rooms

Thin Walls

Stone Cribs

War at Home

Days of Rage

Street Justice

WRITING AS KRIS NELSCOTT

Protectors

ALSO BY KRISTINE KATHRYN RUSCH

THE DIVING SERIES

Diving into the Wreck: A Diving Novel

City of Ruins: A Diving Novel

Becalmed: A Diving Universe Novella

The Application of Hope: A Diving Universe Novella

Boneyards: A Diving Novel

Skirmishes: A Diving Novel

The Runabout: A Diving Novel

The Falls: A Diving Universe Novel

Searching for the Fleet: A Diving Novel

The Spires of Denon: A Diving Universe Novella

The Renegat: A Diving Universe Novel

Escaping Amnthra: A Diving Universe Novella

The Court-Martial of the Renegat Renegades

Thieves: A Diving Novel

Squishy's Teams: A Diving Universe Novel

The Chase: A Diving Novel

Ivory Trees: A Diving Universe Novel

Maelstrom: A Diving Universe Novella

THE FEY SERIES

THE ORIGINAL BOOKS OF THE FEY

The Sacrifice: Book One of the Fey

The Changeling: Book Two of the Fey

The Rival: Book Three of the Fey

The Resistance: Book Four of the Fey

Victory: Book Five of the Fey

THE BLACK THRONE

The Black Queen: Book One of the Black Throne

The Black King: Book Two of the Black Throne

THE QAVNERIAN PROTECTORATE

The Reflection on Mount Vitaki: Prequel to the Qavnerian Protectorate

The Kirilli Matter: The First Book of the Qavnerian Protectorate

Barkson's Journey: The Second Book of the Qavnerian Protectorate

Incident at Serebro Academy: The Third Book of the Qavnerian Protectorate

CATHERINE THE GREAT

A RUSCH CRIME STORY

KRISTINE KATHRYN RUSCH

WMG
PUBLISHING

CATHERINE THE GREAT

ISLAND
TREASURE
MGM
MGM
THE CITY OF
ENTERTAINMENT
LUXOR
EXCALIBUR

At one in the morning on Christmas Day, about the time that Santa was (in theory) trying frantically to complete his annual duties, Brett McHenry got caught on security camera footage shoving a woman into an elevator, then punching her boyfriend in the mouth. McHenry, who would later say he was just celebrating his new status as Most Valuable Player at that year's Sin City College Football Bowl, then got into the elevator, elbowed the woman in the face as she tried to get around him, used his key to get to the hotel's VIP floor, and dragged her off the elevator by her hair.

What happened afterward slid into some kind of dispute, since hotel security caught McHenry standing near the elevator with a handful of hair in his right fist. A blood trail covered the carpet leading to the nearby stairwell. The woman emerged, bleeding profusely from the head and nose, in the lobby, looking like—as one not-so-kind guest put it—a refuge from a zombie movie.

Hotel staff called the police and several ambulances. McHenry and his posse, who had apparently continued to beat the woman's boyfriend, were arrested and shoved into police cars under the neon lights of the hotel's valet parking area.

Even before some not-so-disinterested soul leaked spliced security camera footage to every reputable news and sports outlet in the United States, Catherine Tomlinson of the law firm Easton, Farber, Braun, and Kellog, boarded a private jet in Los Angeles. Even though she'd been awakened at 2:15 a.m., after staying up until midnight to adorn the bright yellow tricycle that her youngest son had coveted with plastic rainbow ribbons jetting out of the handlebars and racing stripes along the wheels while her long-suffering husband ate three of the four cookies left for Santa and chased them down with warm milk, Tomlinson looked court-ready. She wore a black silk suit with a demure skirt that flared slightly about the knees and a pair of matching Louboutin pumps with five-inch heels that often made her, with her six-foot frame, the tallest person in the courtroom.

She didn't have the security footage when she got on the jet and settled into the buttery leather seats, her expandable Coach briefcase taking the seat beside her, but she didn't need that footage. She had the viral videos from the onlookers who'd reacted with shock in the wide hallway around the elevator banks.

Her staff—those in the office and the four on the plane, sitting behind her like good associates—were searching for more damning videos and already sending cease-and-desist letters to the various social media sites, along with personal letters to the sources of the videos themselves.

She knew, as she watched the shaky phone-camera footage, heard the expletives from McHenry and his posse, noted the sound of the blows as they rained on the boyfriend, and tried not to wince at the sickening thud of the girl as she hit the elevator wall, that this was a career-killing moment.

The problem was that McHenry was the most talented football player to come out of any college in the past ten years. He was clearly the Number One draft pick for the upcoming April draft...or he had been until 1 a.m. Pacific time on Christmas Day. He already had a Name, Image, and Likeness deal with one of the leading sports agencies in the world, and they had just inked multimillion-dollar deals with all kinds of brand licensing firms.

Those contracts—and the advances that the kid was due (that the agency was due)—would vanish like Santa's sleigh at dawn on Christmas morning. Still, the damage was clear. A lot of the brand announcements had already gone live in the hours after the blowout win at the Sin City College

Bowl, and now those companies would be on the hook for McHenry's drunken mistakes.

The agency had its own IP attorneys, but Tomlinson wasn't going into Vegas to handle the corporate divorces from McHenry. Those would be relatively easy, considering the morals clauses in the contracts of most very young athletes. No, she was heading to Las Vegas because she was one of the best defense attorneys in the nation—a pit bull whose nickname, Catherine the Great, seemed puny and tiny compared with all of her improbable wins.

She leaned back in the much-too-comfortable seat and waved off the croissants and orange juice the flight attendant brought as a matter of course. Tomlinson didn't even take the coffee, knowing there would be more than enough of it in the hotel suite her firm had on standby in one of the most dangerous cities in the world.

She gave herself a moment, let her own reaction to the online videos wash over her, and permitted herself one short minute to consider her daughter, who, at eleven, was edging into puberty much too fast, and gave herself a tiny half-second of rage.

The firm had never hauled Tomlinson away on Christmas before. She had been in court on Christmas during her first two years, back when she had thought being a public defender was a good idea. Most courts were closed for the holiday, or at least the courts that dealt with the defendants she now represented. She usually worked in

L.A. and could handle the judges there like they worked for her.

But she had gotten this case, not just because of her reputation, but because she was also licensed in Nevada. She had gotten her law degree at the Boyd School of Law at UNLV back when the law school had been newly minted and barely accredited. For that reason (and because she was a good-looking woman), she'd had to prove herself over and over again, taking the California bar and passing on the first try, something none of her colleagues at EFBK had managed to do. Not that it had impressed them much when she decided to move from the PD's office. So she had put off parenting, attained pit-bull status, and had become the firm's not-so-secret weapon on do-not-miss cases, which this one was shaping up to be.

She had made a video of her own in the middle of the night, apologizing to her kids for missing the big morning —the first time ever—and kissing her cookie-stained and quite angry husband before heading out the door with her always-packed carryon, her high-end garment bag, and a pair of athletic shoes hidden in a tote.

She needed the armor of the court-ready clothing, partly because she was going to argue for this pig, and partly because she knew the media would be absolutely brutal.

One more second of rage, and then she set it all aside, leaned her head back, and closed her eyes. Anyone who didn't know her would think she was sleeping, but her staff knew she did her best thinking when she shut out the world.

The videos would only get worse. Unlike many cities on the college football rosters, Vegas was full of cameras and a hungry local media that hated anything that put the city in a bad light. It was also full of temptation for young athletes who had no real adult supervision, maybe for the first time in their lives. Who knew what else might show up in the post-game footage?

So she had media relations to deal with as well as a defendant who was not going to realize that his life had gone from glorious to horseshit in the space of six hours.

"Hey, Cat." The voice belonged to Amari Andersen, the associate she never wanted to lose. Amari had been beside her, unpromoted, for the past six years, gunning for full partner status, and unaware that the person who stood in his way was the woman he worked for.

The seat beside her creaked downward just as sandalwood with a hint of citrus hit her nose. Amari's expensive cologne wasn't offensive per se, but it was stronger than usual, probably because he'd been roused only an hour or so as well. The cologne hadn't had time to fade back to its usual barely-there status.

Tomlinson opened her eyes and did not let her annoyance show. Only Amari had the right to interrupt her thinking sessions. If the other associates had found something critical, they would have tapped Amari and given him the information.

Amari clutched his iPad in his meaty fingers. He was as tall as she was, but broad, and had no neck, just like every other former football player she had ever met. He had escaped the ravages of head injuries and broken bones by ripping his ACL in practice the summer between his high school graduation and his freshman year at UCLA. UCLA let him keep the scholarship (because he had graduated number one in his class at one of the best high schools in the nation), and he had gone on to be one of the most impressive students the school had ever seen.

This morning—and it was morning, much as she wanted to deny it—his brow was furrowed and his chocolate brown eyes looked worried.

She waved the flight attendant over, and said, "I'll take the breakfast now," not because she wanted it, but because she had the feeling she would need the fortification.

Then she nodded at Amari, giving him the go-ahead.

"McHenry turns twenty-one tomorrow," Amari said.

A useful fact. Maybe.

"And he was drunk," Tomlinson said. "Please tell me he was drunk."

"Dunno," Amari said. "We haven't gotten any information on the arrest or the processing."

Tomlinson swore quietly. She had called a buddy of hers from one of the major Las Vegas law firms and sent him to the jail to make sure that McHenry was protected as he was processed, but she had boarded the jet before finding out if her friend had actually managed to arrive.

Vegas courts weren't officially open on Christmas Day, but every official rule could be bent. She just wasn't in the position to do it, and she knew her friend wouldn't extend his hospitality that far.

One of her firm's senior partners was currently reaching out to his contacts in Vegas, seeing if they could get an emergency hearing outside of the eyes of the press.

"All right," Tomlinson said, knowing arrest and processing were momentary dead end. She grabbed one of the croissants and leaned over the tray so she would get no buttery flakes on her suit. "Here's what I need to know now. I need to know if McHenry comes from money."

"I don't think it matters," said Kaitlyn Harbour, the newest associate, from behind them. "The agency is paying our fees."

Amari rolled his eyes. He always allowed himself a moment of unprofessionalism when he knew he wasn't in anyone's line of sight except Tomlinson's, which always put her in a delicate position.

She could smile in response, roll her own eyes, or ignore him entirely.

She decided to ignore. She set the heel of the croissant down, wiped off her hands thoroughly so that she wouldn't get butter or flakes on anything, and grabbed the coffee mug. It was too hot, but she didn't set it down.

"The family money matters," she said to Kaitlyn without turning around. "His sports agency is going to dump this kid as soon as they can figure out how to properly spin the catastrophe. At that point, we have to decide if we want to continue."

"Except the agency hired us," Kaitlyn said, not quite willing to let go.

"They didn't hire us to handle brand awareness, Kaitlyn," Tomlinson said. "They hired us to defend the kid at his arraignment, to see how we can mitigate the damage to his career—"

"He doesn't have a career," muttered David Obi, her other new associate. From the sound of his voice, he was directly behind her.

"Oh, he does right now," Tomlinson said, "and he will always be the MVP of yesterday's game. He will not have a future in the NFL, but he has a present, and we need to mitigate whatever damage this caused for the agency. But we can't forget that this is a young man—"

"Who beat up another young man and slapped a woman around," said Nita Quarles, the second oldest associate. She was going to get herself moved to her own office sometime soon, because there was no holding her back.

"Yes, he did," Tomlinson said, keeping her tone neutral.

"Saying he was drunk won't get him out of any of this," David said.

Amari turned around in his chair so he could see his colleagues. "He's twenty years old. If he was drunk, then someone gave him alcohol. If he was drinking in the hotel or the hotel bar or any neighborhood bars, then—"

"It doesn't work that way in Nevada," Tomlinson said.

"Hotels and bars are not liable for anything caused by the alcohol they serve. Only the drinker themselves and the hosts at a social gathering are liable if the drinker is underage."

That silenced her team. She didn't like it. They were not versed in Nevada law, and they needed to be.

"Then why did you mention his age and ask if he'd been drinking?" Kaitlyn asked, sounding almost pouty.

"Because most people like you," Tomlinson said, "don't know the casinos, hotels, and bars aren't liable. That's the public relations side of this case. We're going to play every single angle as long as this thing is in the news cycle."

Tomlinson had made that kind of speech to her team countless times before. She suspected she would have to give some version of that speech over and over and over again throughout the rest of her career.

The flight attendant scurried over and removed the tray of food. Tomlinson handed her the mug.

At that moment, the jet started its descent into the North Las Vegas Airport. There'd better be a limo waiting, because getting a rideshare this far out would be hard, especially on Christmas morning.

Tomlinson should have specified a landing at Harry Reid International Airport instead of North Las Vegas. She had been thinking of the commuter flight, not the Christmas morning hassles.

The descent made her slightly dizzy, which told her she wasn't quite as bulletproof as she'd hoped. She hadn't had enough sleep, and the whiplash of moving to this case from the joys of the holiday had thrown her off as well.

"But his parents' money…?" Kaitlyn asked. She was a dog with a bone, which was one reason why Tomlinson not only hired her but also put her on the team. "How is that relevant?"

"Because if I like him," Tomlinson said, "I'm going to represent him."

"*Like* him?" Kaitlyn asked, and Tomlinson suspected, without looking behind her, that Kaitlyn was asking for the three other team members. "He punched a man, slammed a woman around, and—"

"He was trained to do it," Tomlinson said.

Someone huffed; the sound of a person who didn't dare disagree with her verbally. It was something she used the call the *law school huff,* which meant *I don't have the verbal chops to go toe to toe with you, but someday I will, and I will then show you the error of your ways.*

"Besides," Tomlinson said calmly, as if none of what she saw on the videos had disturbed her at all, "he's about to lose everything. His friends, his family, his freedom, the career he thought he was going to have, the backing of the public and the media. He has no idea the shitstorm that's going to hit him, and he's, as you pointed out, only twenty. His life, as he knew it, is essentially over. I have empathy for that."

"You *do?*" Kaitlyn sounded shocked. "You saw what he did."

"And I suspect what we'll see will get worse before it gets better," Tomlinson said. "But yes, to answer your question. I don't have to like him to empathize with him. I do, right now, have to defend him. And if any of you can't do that to the best of your abilities, I have no issues with that. What I will have issues with is you telling me *after* we've gotten deep into the case that you can't stomach the guy."

She turned in her seat, not enough to strain the seatbelt, but enough so that she could see the three other members behind her. Amari remained in her peripheral vision.

The three other members were staring at her. David wore his impassive face, the one he usually used in court. His bald head was shiny. He had missed a spot shaving on the right side of his chin, but it was hard to see against his dark skin. He had deep circles under both eyes that gave nothing away.

Nita had her straight black hair pulled into a ponytail. She wore a white sweater one size too big, and pants that still bore some holiday glitter from either a previous sweater or a celebration the night before.

She did not look impassive, but slightly furious. Good. Tomlinson would let Nita handle the anger for all of them. Someone had to.

Kaitlyn, who looked like teenager in her mother's clothes, her blonde hair haphazardly piled on top of her head, was even paler than usual. Tomlinson would have to remind her to put on some makeup and maybe teach her to use foundation because that girl's white skin showed her every mood.

Kaitlyn had her left hand balled into a fist, and was tapping her thumb against her lips, almost as if she was trying to force words back inside her throat.

"Something to say, Kaitlyn?" Tomlinson asked. "Now's the time."

Kaitlyn stopped pounding her fist against her lips and instead bit the cuticle on her thumb. She caught herself, brought her hand down, and held it in place with her right hand.

"I want to learn how to do this," she said. "You're not emotional about it, and I know I shouldn't be, but Jesus, those videos are *awful*."

"They are," Tomlinson said. She wasn't going to offer the defense attorney platitude: *What if you got caught doing something awful? You would need someone like us.*

These four had heard that dozens of times in their careers already, not to mention the half a hundred times someone had said it to them in law school. It wasn't Tomlinson's job to hold their hands.

It was their job to hold her up and get her through this absolutely lovely Christmas day, without letting too much of her personal sarcasm slip out.

"Get used to those videos," Tomlinson said. "We're going to see them hundreds of times in a hundred different contexts."

Amari swore. "We're getting the security footage now," he said, looking at his iPad.

And then the plane landed, bouncing on the uneven runway, in a darkness that only Las Vegas natives understood.

Tomlinson allowed herself a single sigh.

And so it began.

Someone had thought to hire a limo after all, maybe even someone on her team. It waited near the strangely designed white terminal building, the only vehicle present this early in the morning. Several other private jets were parked nearby, all dark, although there were lights in one of the hangars, suggesting someone else was here.

Tomlinson followed her team down the narrow stairs onto the runway, her Louboutins carefully balanced on the metal.

The air was desert cold, dry, and frigid. Tomlinson could see her breath. She hadn't worn a coat, thinking her suit jacket would be enough, but this apparently was one of those icy Christmases that most people didn't know existed in Southern Nevada.

Heels clicked across the tarmac as her team headed to the closed terminal. It had no visible holiday decorations, which did not surprise her. There was probably a desultory tree inside, maybe some kind of holiday greeting posted for the regular travelers who had chosen the smaller neighborhood airport over the larger one in the center of town.

The city itself was decoration enough—lights glinting against the blue-black sky. The Strat dominated the constantly changing skyline, but the Strat was the only familiar thing. The skyline was nothing like the skyline she'd remembered from her childhood, let alone the one she'd seen as little as a year ago.

The limo driver was standing outside, leaning against the hood, smoking. He tossed his cigarette as the team approached, then stomped on it. The nicotine-scented smoke blew toward them in the slight winter breeze.

She waved her team into the limo but stayed outside and checked her phone.

Finally, the texts she'd been waiting for. First, the backdoor dealing had guaranteed an arraignment with someone the firm called "a friendly judge" at ten in the morning.

And second, a curt little summons from Tyrone Ortega, the colleague she'd tapped to babysit McHenry.

Meet me outside the Clark County Jail. Text me the moment you arrive.

He'd sent a pin, marking where he'd be in case she'd forgotten about those little benches that were always curiously empty across from the Justice Center.

She walked over to the limo driver, telling him that there would be three stops—the jail, the hotel, and the rent-a-car place at Reid International. Then she stepped into the limo and made sure the privacy screen was up before briefing her team.

The limo smelled faintly of cigarettes and cleaning fluid. She would have complained, except that her part of the drive would only last maybe five minutes.

She tapped Amari to come with her, Kaitlyn to go to the other airport for a good-sized rental car, and Nita and David to register at the hotel. They'd set up war rooms before, and Tomlinson needed one intact and going when she returned. Since she had almost seven hours before she had to be in court, she was going to prepare properly instead of in some dingy courtesy room at the jail.

After she gave the instructions, she pulled out the tote with her sensible shoes. She removed her Louboutins, stuck them in the tote, and slipped on the practical shoes— her feet almost sighing with relief. Then she stuck her impressive shoes into her briefcase.

Now that she knew she didn't have to go immediately from jail to court, she could save the expensive shoes for the appropriate moment. If she'd had the time, she would have put on a different suit as well.

There was almost no traffic, not in this part of the Vegas Valley, and none near the jail. Her five-minute estimate had been spot-on. The limo pulled in front of the benches, under the watchful eye of ostentatiously placed cameras.

Ortega was standing near one of the benches, hands

tucked in his armpits, shifting from foot to foot. He was barely five-five, and as thin as he had been in college, although he'd upgraded his wardrobe. His silk suit shone in the streetlights. He had cut off his waist-length hair—a nod to his successful defense practice and the preferences of judges everywhere for "neatness," which meant anything that didn't look like 1950s white male attire.

Amari got out of the limo first and held the door for Tomlinson, something she couldn't break him of. He then closed the door as she picked her way over some kind of foul liquid pilling against the curb.

"I don't envy you this one," Ortega said by way of greeting. "I'm billing your firm, by the way."

"I'd expect no less," Tomlinson said.

"And not the friends and family rate," Ortega said.

She hadn't expected the friends and family rate, would, in fact, have argued against it, but she would have thought that the argument would have been tough, like it had been in the past.

She let out a breath. "What happened?"

"He used language I haven't heard in a long time," Ortega said. His deep voice was shaking, and she thought she heard anger underneath it. "He asked for a real attorney."

The language had to be truly rough to upset Ortega.

"I suspect if that's what he wants, I'm not a real attorney either," she said.

"I suspect you're right." Then Ortega nodded at Amari. "Good to see you."

Amari smiled. "You too, from one not-real attorney to another."

"I take it he's still drunk," Tomlinson said, even though she hadn't had any confirmation that McHenry had been drunk.

"Oh, yeah. I prevented the breathalyzer, any DNA swabbing, and anything else I could think of, but they're going to get to it."

She expected as much. The longer they held it off, though, the better. Not for the court case as much as for the publicity.

"I'm not seeing any press," she said.

"Not at the jail," Ortega said. "From what I'm hearing, they're mobbing the hotel, trying to get information. But they don't expect anything here until the 26th."

She set aside the news about the hotel. She was going to have to fight the media on this one, just to get untainted information.

She stored that thought away for later, as a possible argument in McHenry's favor.

"You want to be in on this?" Tomlinson said. "You've already suffered the slings and arrows, and you know your way around the city."

"Hell, no," Ortega said. "Vegas is a small town once you get off the Strip, and I have to see these judges every day.

You just work your magic and fly home, because this one's going to be ugly."

"I suspected as much," Tomlinson said.

"Oh, you haven't suspected this," Ortega said. "It's worse than you could imagine."

She raised her eyebrows. She was Catherine the Great. She was a pit bull. She'd seen things.

But Ortega might not know that, since they didn't practice in the same city, and he hadn't seen the details of what she'd done.

He rocked backwards on his expensive shoes, his mouth a thin line, delivering his news with the ease of a practiced trial lawyer.

"You haven't met Mommy and Daddy yet," he said.

She tilted her head back slightly, trying to parse that news. McHenry was a nearly 21-year-old nearly professional athlete who'd signed NIL deals and had been considered a full adult ever since he turned eighteen. What were his parents…?

And then she understood. Maybe if it hadn't been the middle of her night, she might have anticipated this, but she hadn't. She had to pay more attention because she needed to be on top of her game.

Of course the parents were here. They'd probably been to Sin City College Bowl to see their baby's moment of glory. Which would be his *only* moment of glory, ever, in his entire life.

"Daddy's some bigshot back home," Ortega said, his

voice dry. Apparently, he'd had a run-in with Daddy. "He's flashing his identification. Gotta love Vegas, though. Big fish status from outside the city doesn't mean anything to the folks inside."

"And that's a warning to me too, right?" Tomlinson asked. Not about the parents, but about her status as an attorney.

"Make sure you let the authorities here know you're a native," Ortega said, "and you'll be fine. Now, I'm heading home to a warm shower, a warm bed, and a warm husband. You stay safe."

"You too," she said, and hugged him. She took one step back and put her hands on his shoulders, wishing for once there wasn't a height difference so that this didn't feel like an off-balance power move.

"Thanks," she said. "I mean it. Bill the firm however you want, but I owe you personally for this one."

He raised his carefully plucked eyebrows. He had known her long enough to know that when she said she owed him, she meant it.

Then he grinned.

"Let me know your plans," he said, "because if you're still here tomorrow, there's a restaurant that I've wanted to try for nearly a year now. It'll be our last chance to eat somewhere exclusive until January second."

The reference jolted her. She had forgotten: This city went insane during the stretch between Christmas and New Year's. It was one of the few times of year that the tourists spilled out of their little corridors and into local neighborhoods—not because they wanted to, but because Vegas's myriad hotels filled, and the tourists had to go off-Strip to get prices they could afford.

"I'll let you know," she said, keeping her voice calm and unruffled. She didn't want him to know she had forgotten, even though she did appreciate the heads-up.

Not just because there would be tourists everywhere, but because there would also be press. And cameras. Thousands and thousands and thousands of cameras.

Rules and rules and rules were being broken, as every single person was telling her. Most of those people sounded resentful, from guards to clerks. Tomlinson ignored them. She left their rules and their attitudes to Amari. He stayed up front, talking with the administrators and making sure the team had all of the paperwork.

She was actually grateful when she had to shut off her phone and hand it over to the guard as she went inside the jail. She needed the quiet so that she could think.

The provided room was deeper in the jail than she liked. The guard let her inside and then kept the door open —a nice courtesy—while she awaited her brand-new client.

The open door gave the room a chance to air out the embedded stench of sweat and general body odor. It was a smell that she had never gotten used to, which was one reason why she preferred her high-end clients. Usually, she was able to get them bail before they came into her office, and they could clean up before she spent any time with them.

There hadn't been an arraignment or a bail hearing yet, so of course, she had to see McHenry here. It made her wonder how many people in the Las Vegas court system spent several days over a holiday break in jail, just waiting for the basic courtesies to happen—a thought that hadn't crossed her mind before today. There had been night courts in L.A. when she had been a P.D., so no one got stuck over the holiday.

This room was a beige color that was painted over some institutional green. The table was bolted down, and so were the four chairs. There were handcuff hooks on top of the table for the model prisoner whose handcuffs had some give, and some hooks underneath the table, for the dangerous prisoner who probably shouldn't have been alone with anyone at all.

It would be interesting to see how the guards assessed McHenry.

It took them a half an hour to bring him to her, which seemed like twenty minutes too long. But she'd been practicing that sweet smile—pit bulls were for court, not jails— and she'd nicely thanked the guards who brought him inside the room.

There were two guards, men hired for their size and

general frightful demeanor, but they looked small next to Brett McHenry.

His official stats said he was six-two, but she would have guessed that he was at least six-three. His 235 pounds left him looking lean in the torso, unlike many of his colleagues who were already carrying body fat that they would never lose.

His orange prison garb was too tight across his massive shoulders and too loose around the waist. The pants barely covered his powerful thighs. His feet, visible in his cheap prison sandals, had more black toenails than normal-colored ones.

He hadn't washed up, or maybe they hadn't let him yet. Both sides of his cheeks, closest to his ears, were smeared with something black, which might have been dirt, or it might have been dried blood. His eyes were small, blue, and bloodshot. His crooked nose had been broken at least once.

He had an attempt at a beard, and it was coming in as reddish orange as his prison shirt, but his hair—shaved close to the top of his head—looked blond, a real blond, not something that a twenty-something boy would have done for style or a statement.

His hands were shackled around his waist, and he wore chains on his legs as well. She had looked at the jail's color coding regulations, so she had expected him to show up in orange since he was being accused of being a violent offender, but she hadn't really expected the full shackle.

He apparently had not entered this part of his life without a fight.

The guards shoved him into the chair, using his massive shoulders as leverage to work him into position. Then they shackled his hands under the table.

"Knock twice if you need us," the nearest guard said to her, almost like he expected her to prevent him from leaving.

She nodded once.

"Hey!" McHenry said, as the guards started out. "Hey! Where's my lawyer? I'm not staying here with the assistant. They'll say I did something to her, too."

"That is your lawyer," said the other guard. The word *idiot* was implied.

That guard pulled the door closed with a bang, maybe to make Tomlinson feel nervous. But she'd been in more jails and prisons than she wanted to count, and very little made her nervous. Only one client had, a man whom she had quickly pawned off on an associate, because that client had had crazy eyes—the kind that made her almost queasy.

McHenry didn't have crazy eyes. He had hangover eyes. He clearly had a headache that was probably only going to get worse. He reeked of beer and whiskey with a lovely added tang of urine.

The fact that he didn't smell like vomit told her a few things—he was used to drinking to excess; he hadn't been upset about the violence he had caused in that corridor; and he didn't scare easily.

"You?" he said after the door closed. "You're a lawyer?"

"My name is Catherine Tomlinson," she said. "Your agents hired me."

"My *agents?*" he repeated. "Not the team?"

"Your agents," she said, keeping her voice level. She had not yet sat down because she wanted to see how he handled being alone with a woman.

"I need a defense attorney," he said.

"I am a defense attorney," she said and she did not add *One of the best in the country* because it was obvious that a statement like that would provoke the kid rather than prove to him that she was qualified. "I've been hired to get you arraigned and out on bail."

"It's Christmas," he said. "Courts usually aren't open on Christmas."

She kept her expression impassive, even though she didn't like the statement, especially coming from a young defendant.

"And how do you know that?"

"My dad's a defense attorney," McHenry said. This time, the word *proper* was implied. Or maybe the word he had left out was *real*. As in a *real* defense attorney.

"Hm," she said, not committing to anything. But that explained why Daddy had been flashing his credentials, trying to get into the jail, and maybe it explained why Ortega had laughed.

Tomlinson had heard *bigshot* but hadn't figured that the word was connected to *defense attorney*.

"I want him to defend me," McHenry said.

"We'll deal with that after the arraignment," Tomlinson said.

"I'm the client. I want it *now*."

"And I'd like to be home with my kids," Tomlinson snapped. "Neither of us will get what we want. Your father is not licensed to practice in Nevada, or he would have been inside this jail already. I am. I've already moved mountains so that we can get you out of here today. If you'd like to slow things down, see if your dad can find someone with a Nevada law license who will work with him, and a judge who's willing to take you on during this hectic week, no worries. I'll step away. As you said, you're the client."

The kid's small eyes shot from side to side. He tried to raise a hand, and instead banged the underside of the table, but he didn't wince. It was almost as if he didn't feel anything.

"My father went to Harvard," he said, probably parroting his father's own statements about his qualifications for various cases.

"Last I checked, Harvard is on the East Coast," she said. "But if you think someone who has received a law degree in another state would do better for you, that's your choice. I will step away."

Then his gaze met hers. His expression was hostile, but his eyes were feral. No wonder he was good on the field.

Just a glare from those eyes would make the average college football player quake in his pampered little boots.

She didn't quake. She'd seen worse. Granted, she'd seen it from older men who'd had more years to practice that look, but still. Very little intimidated her anymore, certainly not a twenty-year-old fuck-up who still hadn't realized his old life was over.

"All right," he said, as if he was giving her a gift. "What can you do for me?"

"I'm going to do my best to get you arraigned and out of here before the press show up," she said.

Those small eyes widened. He hadn't thought of the press.

"Believe me," she said, "they're interested. You've already gone viral, and not in a good way."

He let out a gusty breath. The mention of the press was the first thing that had broken through his shell.

"What about my posse?" he asked.

"Your accomplices?" She leaned on the word hard. "Because that's what the prosecutors will call them. Accomplices."

He frowned, and she had a hunch that if he could have, he would have waved a hand at her, demanding that she continue.

"Your…accomplices," she said, "they went viral too, but not like you. They didn't just tank a career that could have made them tens of millions of dollars in the next five years."

"What?" The frown had left. Now he was perplexed. This pampered kid had no idea what he had done, and it was her job to give him as many clues as she could.

She needed him to be humble and remorseful by the time he hit court, and she wasn't sure that even her mighty skills could make that happen in the time remaining.

"You want to tell me what that girl did to you?" she asked.

"What girl?" he responded, and he wasn't being cute. He clearly didn't know what she was talking about.

"The girl you shoved into an elevator so hard that it sounded like you'd broken her. The girl whom you dragged off that elevator by her hair. The girl who somehow escaped you and fled, showing up in the lobby, bloody and in tears. That girl."

His frown had returned. For a moment, she wondered if she was dealing with a blackout drunk. She could argue that, make it work, at least for bail.

He blinked, as if he was trying to remember, and then he let out a sigh. "That girl. Shit, who knew she'd be a whiny little bitch."

It was all Tomlinson could do not to close her eyes.

"You mean you've treated other women like that?" she asked.

His eyes narrowed. "Are you sure you're my attorney? Because you don't fucking sound like it. All you women, you cluster together and squawk. I'd like a different attorney. A proper one. A man."

"A white man," she said, her voice calm.

"That would be better," he said. "And older, too. Someone who actually knows what they're doing."

"All right," she said. "I'll make a note for your agency to assign you someone else, preferably white and male. I'm sure they'll get back to you after the holidays."

She pivoted, glad she hadn't sat down, and headed for the door. She was about to pound her fist on it when the kid said, "Wait!"

She waited, hand still balled in a fist, poised to knock on that door. She did not turn around.

"You're not kidding about the timeline, are you?" He sounded almost reasonable.

She still didn't turn, but she did drop her arm. "I'm not kidding about the timeline."

"Tell me about it," he said.

She didn't like the tone. It still had too much of an air of command. She wondered how this kid managed to play on a team filled with players of color and cooperate with them. Maybe because the coach had been a *real* coach, paunchy and middle-aged, male and white. As had most of his staff.

If she left now, the dismissal would be on her, and this whiny kid would say that she had left him. So, she turned around.

He looked younger than he had a moment ago, and the feral look had left his eyes. Maybe he was just beginning to realize how much trouble he was in.

"This is Las Vegas," she said. "And it's Christmas. Usually, the courts aren't in session, but we managed to find a friendly judge to preside over your arraignment. That courtesy will vanish when I walk out that door."

The kid leaned back just a little. The handcuff chain rattled as he moved. He was listening now.

"If you decide to go with your father, it will take until January second to get an attorney in place. No one likes working the week between Christmas and New Year's. Most trial dates are set. Arraignments happen, but you'll get a local attorney, whoever happens to be around." She gave him her coldest smile. "You met my colleague who works here, Tyrone Ortega. Apparently, you didn't think he was a real attorney either, so I can guarantee that he won't take your case. He's professional, so he won't tell anyone what you said to him besides me and my team, which he's a part of."

The kid's skin was going a ghostly white.

"There are some very good defense attorneys here in Las Vegas," she said. "They've handled a lot of high-profile cases. But they won't get on board fast enough to prevent the media circus that will surround you shortly. Nor will they want to use their clout to force a judge to hear your case today. They don't know you. I know them, though. They're not motivated by money. They want a case they can win, or at least mitigate. This is not that case, not for them."

"What?" the kid asked. "What do you mean?"

She was surprised. He hadn't thought it through. Or maybe, if she thought about it, she wasn't surprised after all. He was very young.

She kept her tone cool, detached, a bit sarcastic. "The press already has the security footage from the hotel. Videos of the incident have already gone viral. Your best chance is to be arraigned today, and maybe, if the judge truly is a friendly, you'll get to go home to wherever you live in Dixieland."

She hadn't picked that word intentionally, and as soon as it left her mouth, she flagged it. She couldn't let the sarcasm or her difficulties with this kid get in her way.

"Otherwise," she said, "you'll be arraigned sometime this week. Maybe tomorrow, maybe later, depending on the clout of your attorney. With each passing second, the media—both the mainstream sports media and those opinionated folk on social media—will define you and your case."

"They'll do that anyway," he said. This time, he didn't speak with bravado. He sounded subdued.

"Yes, they will," she said, "but as I said, we can mitigate it. If you post bail and fly back to..." *whatever hell hole you came from,* she edited out before she spoke it "...your parents' house, then we have people who can cast doubt on the possible charges. 'See?' our people will say. 'It can't be that bad if the judge let him leave the State.'"

"Will that happen?" he asked.

"I have no idea," she said. "It will depend on a thousand

things, including your comportment in court today, if indeed you go today. What you need to understand is that every state has peculiarities and different laws and unwritten rules. I know Nevada."

Although not as well as she wanted to; she would need local help if she pursued this case after next week.

"Your father doesn't know Nevada at all. I know you're used to listening to him, but he will not be your best advocate in this case, even if he gets a Nevada attorney to sit beside him."

"You don't like my father," the kid said.

"I've never met your father," she said, "but I can tell you this: He has a major conflict of interest. You're his son. That fact will cloud his judgment."

"Not his." The kid sounded bitter.

She held up her hands. She was done here. "Good luck," she said, and headed for the door.

"Wait!" the kid said one more time. "I want to go to court today."

She suppressed a sigh. "It's the sensible move."

"You'll handle that, right?" he asked.

"I'll handle that," she said. "But I'm not going to promise that I'll handle anything else."

"That's okay," he said. "I'm not sure I want you to."

She raised one single eyebrow, making sure there was contempt on her face.

"I-I-I mean," he stammered, "it depends on how well you do."

"How well *I* do?" she asked.

"I mean, y'know, if you win."

His worldview was narrow, his mind even more so.

She crossed her arms, paused, then gathered herself.

"There is no winning here, Brett." She sounded surprisingly gentle, even to her own ears. Maybe she did have a bit of empathy for him after all. He was clearly over his head. "You lost the moment you shoved that girl into the elevator."

His chains rattled. He shook them in frustration, his face getting red. Then he settled back down.

"I don't know what you mean," he said.

She paused again, wondering how much she should reveal. Then she decided to let him know, so that he understood. He was a kid, yes, but in the eyes of the law, he was an adult who made his own choices.

"I am a defense attorney," she said, even though she had already told him that. "Keep that in mind. I will be paid by your sports agency no matter how I do. Keep that in mind as well. I'm here to do the best I can for you. Keep that in mind."

He shifted, cheeks getting redder. She was getting a sense that people rarely talked to him like this.

"The best for you, today," she said, "is to get you home, as I mentioned. You need to get out of Nevada, and you need to do it quietly. You should not engage with the press once you get free from this state. You should not talk about the case. You most certainly should not call one of the victims *a whiny little bitch*. Or any other name. Is that clear?"

He bit his lower lip, his face getting redder, his eyes getting smaller. She couldn't quite tell if they were filled with tears or not.

"You committed a vicious assault on camera. It doesn't matter what your defense attorney argues at your trial—and there will be a trial—a year from now. What matters at the moment is getting you as close to free as possible and turning the media's attention to something else."

He was shaking now, and it certainly wasn't with cold. This smelly little room had gotten hot.

"On that matter, we might be lucky if we play our cards right." She almost smiled at her own Vegas metaphor, but she didn't. She wanted him to listen. "This is a holiday week. While that works against you as a defendant, it works for you as the subject of a juicy sports story. Attention spans are short. Other games are getting played. Right now, very few people are even looking at social media. They're doing holiday things, which they will be doing all week."

He sat up just a bit straighter, as if he needed to do that to hear her better.

"But, if you persist in calling people names or talking to the press, then you will remain a story, even in these quiet days, *especially* in these quiet days, because most sports fans will be watching football in their leisure hours, and if the games are dull or if there's too much downtime, the sportscasters will be talking about what's in the news. If you put yourself front and center in the news, then you'll be the subject of conversation."

His eyes were filling with tears. She was getting through.

"And," she said, "it won't be good conversation. Your position as the MVP of the Sin City College Football Bowl will get mentioned over and over again, as will your talent on the field, but only in the *isn't it too bad he threw it all away* sense."

He winced.

"Do you really want to be the subject of that discussion in the next few weeks?" she asked.

He blinked, one tear escaping and loosening some of the dirt on his cheek. Then he swallowed.

"That doesn't sound like something a defense counsel should be worried about," he said. "It sounds like something someone who works for PR worries about."

A surge of anger ran through her, but she kept it down.

"You can ask your father this one," she said. "Half of defending a client—any client—is handling the media. The media influences juries. Juries can't unhear a story that got pounded into them over and over again during that holiday lull."

"First," he said, "you're assuming I'll go on trial. Second, you can select the biased ones out."

She wasn't going to argue the law with him. This kid was astonishingly pigheaded, which she should have expected. Behavior didn't change just because someone got a talking to.

"You're right. You might not go on trial," she said. "But you will get charged with several felonies, and they were caught on security video. The best we're going to be able to do is plead you down to some lesser charge—what, I don't know yet. Judging from what I'm seeing today, you're not going to plead. If you don't plead, you'll go on trial."

"If we plead," he said, sounding a bit wobbly, "can we put this away by the draft in April?"

His complete lack of understanding caught her off guard. He had no idea what kind of trouble he was in.

Or maybe he did.

She suddenly put the pieces together. Father—defense attorney; son—football star; major university sports program; alumni money; complicit cops. This kid had been in trouble before. Maybe big trouble.

And everyone had looked the other way or had been actively complicit in keeping his crimes silent.

She had two instant reactions to that thought. The first startled her. She wanted this case. She wanted it badly. It would be one of the toughest cases she had ever handled, and she wanted to win it to cement her own reputation.

The second was a lot more nuanced. In her mind, she kept hearing the meaty thud of that girl's head against the back of the elevator, saw the clutch of hair in his hands, and she knew if this thing went to trial, she'd have to destroy that poor girl on the stand.

What kind of example would that be to her daughter?

"I can't answer that question properly," Tomlinson said, "until I know exactly what the charges are."

"You said the judge is a friendly," the kid said, pushing.

"Not the kind of friendly you're used to," she said, and left it at that.

She left shortly after that without asking him anymore about the assault, the girl, or the guy who got kicked by McHenry's so-called posse. Tomlinson was taking this one moment at a time. This moment? Get through the day. She was going to figure out what was best for this client, and that would take more doing than she had thought.

When she got her phone back, she still didn't look at her texts. Instead, she called her team as she walked, ordering someone to pick her up outside the jail in ten minutes.

She asked for ten minutes, because she already knew what would be waiting for her by the door.

Brett McHenry's father looked like an older, meaner version of his son. The older McHenry wasn't as bulky, but he was also missing a neck, which meant he'd played football once in the distant past as well. He was balding, but what remained of his hair was the same odd blond that she had seen on his son.

McHenry moved toward her as she came out of the

doors leading into the jail, as if she had no idea who he was. He was obvious, but she wouldn't have known who his wife was had she stepped forward, because she looked like she had nothing to do with her son's genetics—until she raised her head.

She had the same small eyes, a pale blue that could look right through anyone who got in her way. She wore a bright Alexander McQueen iris blazer, an inappropriate white with an inappropriate design of an eye that ran from shoulder to hip. She was thin enough to look okay in the blazer, but the white seemed like a prayer to a summer that had long fled. She had paired the blazer with a black silk skirt that showed off thin, muscled legs and knobby knees.

She had to be cold, but she didn't look it. Nor had she gotten a speck of dirt on that blazer, which had to be some kind of miracle.

"Ms. Tomlinson," McHenry said as he stationed himself directly in front of her. "I'm Bartholomew McHenry. You've been tasked with representing my son. I would like to talk with you about that."

His voice was low and controlled, but it carried. His black suit was silk, just like hers, and fit perfectly. He looked like the expensive lawyer his son had made him out to be.

"I'm afraid I can't say much to you, Mr. McHenry," Tomlinson said. "I'm your son's lawyer, not yours."

"I understand that," he said with just a bit of contempt. "But perhaps you have no idea who I am. I'm also a defense attorney. I have made it a practice to represent many athletes. I've been called on by various universities and some professional sports teams to do important defense work, because dealing with athletes and the justice system is a particular skill—"

"I understand that, sir," she said, mimicking his tone. "I have also been informed that you've been here most of the night, so you probably did not have time to look up anything about me. I suggest that you do so. Not that it matters. I have spoken to your son. I will be representing him in the preliminary parts of this case. He will decide after the arraignment about his choice of counsel going forward."

"I would like you to sit second chair," the older McHenry said. "I will handle this case, and you can monitor Nevada law for me."

She stared at him for a moment, making sure she held eye contact. He didn't break eye contact, even though she half expected it. Instead, he raised his chin just enough to make it clear to her that she actually had an inch or two of height on him.

They could have a staring contest all day or she could get out of here. Without breaking eye contact, she said, "I spoke to your son about his options, including having his famous father defend him. Your son has chosen me to represent him for the arraignment. As I said, he might make other choices after that. But for now, I am his attorney of record."

She started to walk past McHenry, but the older man stepped in front of her, blocking her again. This time, he also took a step too close, a move designed to make her uncomfortable.

"I will represent my son," McHenry said.

"That may be so in the future," Tomlinson said. "But under the law, your son is a full adult. Choice of counsel is your son's choice, not yours. Now, if you'll excuse me, I have a case to prepare for."

"You can't," McHenry said. "You will—"

"Mr. McHenry." She finally raised her voice enough to get the attention of one of the guards nearby. He started toward them, but she raised a hand, stopping him. "I need to know something. How many times have you represented your son in a court of law?"

"In court?" McHenry said. "Never."

He seemed proud of that. Which was as she expected.

"Let me rephrase," she said. "How many times have you defended your son against difficult charges?"

McHenry's eyes narrowed. "I don't see how that's relevant."

"It's relevant," she said, "because your son has an unreasonable expectation that what might possibly be a series of felony assault charges will just disappear."

"A good attorney can make that happen," McHenry said, his voice getting tight.

"Maybe in a small college town where the police and the judges are known to be people who root for the local team, maybe even people who have a lot of money invested in the university and its sports programs." She deliberately looked down on him. "Your son chose to commit these acts of violence in Las Vegas, land of security cameras, a place where you know no one and have no connections."

"It's not hard to get someone who has connections," he said.

"Maybe in the places you practice law," she said, "but here things are different. Las Vegas is not the town that you have heard about in movies and on the news. This place threw the mob out decades ago and has worked very hard to clean up its act. The anti-corruption statutes have teeth, and the judges abide by them, as do the local attorneys—"

"Except that you're not local, Ms. Tomlinson." McHenry's cheeks were slightly dotted with red. She was making him angry. "I did look you up. You're with some California firm, but you're not a named partner."

So, apparently, he was, probably in some tiny firm that no one had ever heard of.

"Ah, but I am local, sir," she said. "I was born and raised here. I went to law school here, which doesn't match your Harvard degree, I know, but what it means is that I'm exceedingly well-versed in Nevada law. I am based in California because my firm is based there, and I am licensed there as well because, despite the relative newness of UNLV's law school, my education was solid enough for me to pass the California bar on my very first attempt."

She hadn't planned to haul that out, but he might have been making her angry as well.

"I started working on your son's case at two a.m. this morning, and I still have a lot of preparation to do." She smiled thinly. "So, stand aside. I have a job to do, and you're getting in the way."

"You don't need to do a lot of prep," McHenry said. "He's a star. He needs star treatment."

She gave him one of her vicious courtroom smiles, the one she used for particularly stupid people on the stand.

"Correction, Mr. McHenry," she said. "He *was* a star, until one o'clock this morning when he made some very bad decisions. He—"

"He can remain a star if you handle this correctly," McHenry said.

"Las Vegas is not some college town with the police its pocket," she said. "By Las Vegas standards, your son isn't a star. He's a kid with a dream. Now, if you'll excuse me."

She pushed past him, actually bumping his shoulder. The wife started to move into Tomlinson's path, but Tomlinson gave her a glare that she rarely used outside of court.

The wife stopped moving and tugged nervously on the hem of her Alexander McQueen.

Neither of them tried to block Tomlinson. The room behind her got quiet as the door opened, and she stepped out into the cold.

The sky was getting lighter. She would have thought

that dawn had already broken, because it felt like she had spent three days inside. But her watch told her it hadn't been that long.

Bless her staff, they had a car waiting for her. The street was empty, but Amari was still standing outside the vehicle, just to make sure she knew the car was for her.

She wondered if his quest to get all the necessary forms and documents had been successful.

"How's the client?" he asked.

"We'll talk about it at the hotel," she said.

"And the infamous parents?" he asked.

"The root cause of the problem," she said, and let herself into the car's back seat.

Las Vegas always built new hotels, and fortunately for the Tomlinson team, this year's crop had been built on the North Strip, a ten-minute drive from the courthouse. The hotels were large enough to have hundreds of suites, and her company was willing to pay a small fortune to commandeer one, even at the prices being charged for the week that Vegas called NYE.

The suite was on the 65th floor, which wasn't quite the top, but close enough. The suite was large enough to have its own private elevator. David, who had picked them all up, handed both Amari and Tomlinson their own keys to the suite and informed them that the keys also operated the elevator.

This hotel was newer and larger than the hotel where Brett McHenry had committed assault, but Tomlinson eyeballed the elevator anyway. She still wasn't sure whether or not she would defend the kid after today, but just in case, she wanted a few things on the record.

"Someone get me the measurements for the elevator where the incident took place," she said. "Something accurate. I want to know how much force he had to use to send that girl against the far wall."

Dave was making notes in his iPad, nodding as he did so. "You want the area outside of the elevator, too, right?"

"Yeah," she said. "I also want as many photos as you can get. I know that the media has some, and there were viral videos, but I want our own photographs of the area where the assault occurred. I also want to know if there is or was a blood trail near that elevator, across that upper floor—whatever one it is—and down the hallway. Let me know how far that poor girl had to run to get to the stairs. And get me her name."

"Her name is Keesha Orille," Amari said quietly. "She's going to press charges."

Good, Tomlinson thought, but didn't say. It wasn't good for their client, but she was personally glad the girl was going to stand up for herself.

Or the girl might, until the father offered her money.

She let out a sigh.

"We're going to need to get someone to keep an eye on those parents," she said, as the elevator stopped its rapid upward ascent. "I don't want any of you to do it, nor do I want that horrid couple anywhere near our operation. In fact, I don't want them to know anywhere we're working. Is that clear?"

"Yes," David said as the doors started to open.

"You afraid they'll do something untoward?" Amari asked. Or maybe that wasn't a question. Maybe that was a statement.

"I'm afraid they'll pay off the witnesses. So get someone on them. I don't care if they're followed or if someone decides to babysit them. But I need it to happen, and I need it to last all day."

"What about after our court hearing?" Amari asked. He understood what she was doing. "You're not taking this case?"

"All day encompasses after the court hearing," Tomlinson said. "I'll make a decision at that point."

Then she stepped out of the elevator into a suite so new it still smelled like carpet glue. The entry was the size of an entry in a regular hotel corridor. Two different hallways snaked out of the entry. One hallway curved slightly straight ahead; the other went to the right.

It was clear that the designers of the suite meant for most people to go forward, not to the right, so she figured the suite's kitchen, and its bedrooms were off to the side.

David got off the elevator and immediately went for the

wider curved hallway, confirming her suspicion. She followed him, past the expensive prints behind frames that were not attached to the walls. Apparently, the assumption was that whoever stayed in this suite could afford to replace any artwork that was stolen or damaged.

A half-bath opened on the left, followed by another curve, and then she was in the suite's main room, not that she noticed much about it immediately. Large windows covered the entire wall across from her and curved toward her right and toward her left, showing the Vegas Strip and the mountains in Summerlin, with the city sprawled beneath them.

Her first thought was that even though this view was spectacular, it had been designed for nighttime viewing, all twinkling lights and gaudy bright cityscapes.

She had to make herself look away to take in the room. It was large enough to dwarf the grand piano that was placed against the left wall, with a furniture grouping around it for ease of listening. Another grouping, with a full sofa and matching chairs, was in front of her, and yet another grouping was on the wall on her right, with chairs for serious discussions.

Impressive enough, even for people who had never been in an upscale suite.

"Where's the war room?" she asked, because this clearly wasn't it.

"This way." David threaded his way through the furniture groupings on the right to a faux hallway, made by furniture and windows, acting as a funnel to the necessarily hidden parts of the suite.

She followed him, more astonished than she wanted to be about the size of this place. Vegas was always about big, bigger, biggest, but this—which wasn't even the grandest suite in the hotel—was much larger than she expected.

The faux hallway opened into a dining room with a table that easily sat twelve, an actual bar on the inside wall, and a glimpse of the kitchen beyond.

David kept going to a smaller hallway without any windows. He stepped through a door. She followed.

The conference room was as big as the one in her California law office. It could seat twenty people if need be. Fortunately, it did not have any windows, because whoever had designed this had designed it for business people.

The expensive artwork—if there had been any—had been removed from the walls, and her team had affixed white boards, maps, and more papers than she realized they had already generated.

She stood at the head of the table, put her hands on her hips, and stared at their work, seeing no flaws. She also saw things she absolutely did not like, things that would make defending the younger McHenry very difficult if this case got to court.

"I assume we've been in contact with social media sites about quashing the early viral videos," she said. When she spoke like this, her team had to know that she thought such steps were the obvious ones. If they hadn't done it, they would be braced for some kind of tongue-lashing.

"Most have cooperated," Nita said. She was standing closest to the door. Her shoes were off, her bare feet sunk deep into the plush carpet. She had shadows underneath her nutbrown eyes, but she seemed like a woman with a great deal of energy.

Which was good, because they had only just begun to do the job.

She added, "Twitter is the usual problem, as are some of the smaller and newer sites. I contacted the team back in California to handle this as swiftly as possible."

The team in California was a part of the IT division, filled with lawyers who had a myriad of social media experience, and knew who to contact to get things done. The team also knew how far the threat of lawsuit could push each individual social media site. Some reacted appropriately to those threats; others reacted publicly and made the situation worse.

"I've been told," Nita said, "that we are lucky this incident happened in the middle of our night. The videos aren't as viral as they would have been had this happened right after the game. Fortunately, the rest of the world does not care about American Football."

She said that with enough disdain to show that she didn't really care about it either.

"Any estimates on how many people saw it?" Tomlinson asked as she set her briefcase down near the door.

"We could get a guess, but nothing yet because I didn't ask for it." Nita was always up front about what she was doing, even if she thought Tomlinson would disagree with her methods. "I'll be honest with you, though. I'm not liking what I'm seeing."

"Tell me," Tomlinson said.

"Better to show you," Nita said.

She picked up a clicker, and a screen came down over the wall directly across from Tomlinson. Nita tapped the keyboard on her laptop, and an image appeared on the screen.

It was from the security footage. It showed Brett McHenry standing next to the elevator, clutching a fistful of hair. Something dripped off the hair, probably blood. The girl—Keesha—had her back to him, a bare foot vulnerably and nakedly visible, as she clearly ran away from him.

Tomlinson suppressed a sigh. She would have to compare the girl's clothing from before the shove into the elevator to after she got out on whatever floor that was.

Above the photo was the breathtakingly awful sentence, *When did scalping become part of a post-game celebration?*

Of course the person who posted was hidden behind a handle that didn't reveal their real identity, although some of the responses that scrolled through showed some average people, at least one of whom noted that scalping had become a white trick in the Old West to make it seem like the various Native American tribes were more blood-thirsty than they actually were.

"Tell me you got that taken down," Tomlinson said.

"Oh, we did," Nita said, "but you know the internet. It's not gone forever."

Tomlinson nodded. That image was a confirmation that this job was going to be as hard as she thought it would be.

Maybe she'd show that to Daddy Dearest if he gave her any more trouble. She would wager he hadn't had to deal with problems like this in his entire career.

"Did we find out who leaked the security footage yet?" she asked.

"The hotel tracked the internal suspect immediately. The idiot was still on the job in their security room. He'd taken pictures of the security images with his phone."

"I thought hotel security people weren't allowed to have phones in their rooms," Tomlinson said. It had been that way here in Vegas since the dawn of cell phones.

"Some of the older hotels are lax in their security measures," Nita said. "They're no longer used to handling high-profile clients."

"Great." Sometimes being a Vegas native was a problem. Tomlinson could remember when the hotel where the incident had taken place had been built. Back then, the hotel had been as upscale as this one.

"They fired him," Nita said, "but that's not going to matter. He probably got paid a small fortune for selling the video last night."

"And we've got someone who is going to take that small fortune away from him, right?" Tomlinson asked.

"Yes," Nita said. "We've got one team on quashing and one team on suing. As soon as we get information, we send it back to California, and the teams take over."

As it should be on a case like this. Tomlinson knew her billable hours were going to include a holiday sacrifice rate. She didn't want to know what the bill just for today was going to be to the agency. It was probably going to be at least a million.

They wouldn't mind, either, if her firm made this problem mostly disappear.

She wished the offensive image and its offensive caption would disappear too, but as she had told the team, she would have to get used to it just like they would.

"Anyone want to tell me how that kid got so much hair in his hands?" she asked. She needed to know how bad the assault was.

"They're extensions," Nita said quietly.

Tomlinson caught herself before she raised a hand to her own scalp. She'd been known to wear extensions from time to time. If they were attached properly, they were affixed with a special adhesive. Whenever she'd gotten her extensions, her stylist reminded her not to remove them herself.

People go to the hospital for that, her stylist would add.

Which, apparently, young Keesha had. And maybe for more.

"That explains the blood on her face," Tomlinson said. "Head wounds bleed a lot."

"Some of that is from her nose as well," Amari said from slightly beside her. "He broke it."

"This kid is charming," Tomlinson said.

"It gets worse." Amari handed her one of the documents he'd collected. It was the original police report, which listed not just the hair-yanking and the broken nose, but a concussion from that hit against the elevator wall. And those were just the wounds to the girl's head.

Tomlinson made sure that she didn't change her expression as she read the not-quite-dispassionate prose.

Victim hard to understand due to lost teeth.

Tomlinson had expected crying, but the report did not list that.

Spiral fracture of the right wrist, the report continued. *Bruising visible on legs and thighs consistent with claims of sexual assault.*

And then this:

Victim could not defend herself because the initial blow had caused her to momentarily black out. When she awakened, she found the Subject on top of her. She managed to grab his privates and twist, making him back away. Then she crawled to the control panel, unlocked the elevator, and got it to the next floor, where the subject hit her again, took her to his floor, and dragged her by her hair into the corridor. Victim managed to escape, leaving Subject with a handful of her hair...

Tomlinson handed the report back to Amari. She didn't need to see more to understand several things.

The younger McHenry was quick and efficient, brutal

and self-serving. His athletic training had probably made him capable of committing several actions at the same time and keeping track of all of them.

The girl, Keesha, had been lucky to get away.

Tomlinson wondered how many others had not been.

Her stomach was twisting, but she didn't want her staff to see that this had disturbed her. So, she stood, just like she would have in court, and asked, "How many networks have the security video?"

"All of them," Nita said.

Of course they did, which Tomlinson should have known.

"Let me rephrase. How many of them have run the security video?"

"Only one so far," Nita said. "One of the sports channels which has a full team here in Vegas. They got secondary confirmation that the security video is accurate. The others were a lot later in trying to get confirmation, and the hotel shut down any discussion of what happened at our request."

Or maybe, at the threat of lawsuit from the team back in California.

Whatever worked.

"No one else is playing it right now," Nita said. "The original station stopped playing it about an hour ago."

"Good," Tomlinson said. "Let's keep it that way. And we'll need someone to make sure this police report stays under wraps as well."

"Already on that," Amari said. "I started that discussion this morning, reminding Las Vegas Metro that our client is innocent until proven guilty and that we're a very big, very powerful law firm."

Tomlinson smiled at him. She had known how Amari had done this as if she had been beside him. He had a polite, non-aggressive manner that made any threat he actually made seem all the more real.

"I don't think we have a lot to worry about there though," he said. "Much, much, much bigger fish have gone through that police department, and their reports didn't leak. This kid is a bit player as far as Las Vegas is concerned."

One of the few things that worked in the kid's favor.

Tomlinson nodded. Then she ran fingers over her eyes. "Someone show me which room is mine. I'm going to need a moment to freshen up after my time in that jail."

No one questioned it. Her "moment to freshen up" was distant enough from her reading of the police report to keep her reaction to it her own personal secret.

David led her down yet a different hallway, which connected, apparently, to the one on the right near the elevators. This suite was so big that a person could literally get lost in it.

Her own room was the largest, of course, with its own sitting area which was the size of her own living room at home, a private bath, and a bedroom that was toward the back. The sitting area had a lovely view of the cityscape and the mountains.

"Thanks," she said to David, and closed the door. Then she leaned on it.

Her impression of the kid hadn't been wrong. The words feral and vicious had come to mind when she had seen him the first time, and he was certainly that.

He was also clearly a serial offender, or he wouldn't have had that elevator routine down pat.

She had no idea why he had initiated the attack, and she probably needed to know that, but she also knew he wouldn't tell her. The answer was probably in the posse's takedown of the young man outside the elevator.

She would look that up in a minute.

She made her way to the nearest chair and sank into it. Pinkish light was covering the mountains, showing that dawn had finally hit the Valley.

Dawn was when her kids usually got up on Christmas morning. She could call them right now, maybe even watch their celebration on Zoom, but she didn't want to. Not because she didn't want to see them—she did—but because she didn't want her older kids and her husband to see her right now.

They would immediately know something was wrong.

When she had taken the job at Easton, Farber, Braun, and Kellog, her mentor, Suzette Carmichael, a judge on U.S. District Court for the Central District of California, had told her that she would eventually come across a case that might make her question everything.

It's not all about winning and losing, Cat, Suzette had said. Defense attorneys see the worst of humanity and must figure out how to defend that behavior. At some point, someone will do something that offends you on such a deep level that you're going to wonder why you're doing what you're doing. However, you will still owe that client the best possible defense. It is, emotionally, one of the most difficult positions to be in.

Tomlinson thought she had already encountered those emotional and ethical dilemmas, but she now realized she hadn't. She had steered away from serial murder cases and those rabid-eyed defendants who set their neighbors on fire by defending high-profile clients. She had never run into someone like Brett McHenry, although she had known it was possible.

She just hadn't expected it to make her nauseous. Maybe the proximity of this defense and the loss of Christmas morning with her children made her a little more sensitive.

Or maybe she was just hungry. She hadn't really eaten much.

She stood up, grabbed her go-bag, and went into the bedroom. There she changed into a UNLV Rebels sweatshirt and a pair of sweatpants, carefully hanging her suit in the closet. She didn't need to get it more wrinkled than it already was.

She went into the oversized and too-bright bathroom, splashed water on her face, and leaned forward.

She already knew she was done with this kid. She couldn't cross-examine Keesha Orille on the stand when this thing went to trial.

But Tomlinson still had to offer Brett McHenry the best possible defense today.

She patted her face with a plush white towel, then hung it back on the rack. Then she went back to the conference room.

Everyone on her team was standing, each doing something different. Kaitlyn was making sure the computer notes were in order, using their portable scanner to upload the police report. Amari was adding to the timeline on one of the whiteboards while David appeared to be typing that in.

Nita was pacing in the back of the room, apparently giving orders to whoever had the misfortune to work at the firm on Christmas Day.

"Someone order room service breakfast," Tomlinson said. "I want us all to eat hearty fare, since I have no idea when we will eat next, and we need to be fortified. Get lots of coffee—hotel coffee, because I'm not sending anyone on a Starbucks run."

"They can deliver, too," Kaitlyn said.

"Okay, then you're in charge of that and all the food," Tomlinson said. "I need it here within the next half an hour."

Kaitlyn nodded and grabbed the house phone. As she did, David slid into her seat to take over the documents upload.

"Who liaised with McHenry's hotel?" Tomlinson asked.

"I did," David said, holding one of the documents that Amari had gotten in his right hand.

"I need you to talk with them again. Find out the names of everyone they released the security footage to," Tomlinson said.

Nita hung up and joined the conversation. "I already found out who the guard sold the footage to."

"Which you gave to the folks back in LA," Tomlinson said. "I want to know who the hotel gave the footage to. That includes the footage in the valet parking area as well."

"I'm on it," David said. He got up from the upholstered seat, grabbed his cell phone, and stepped into the hallway.

Amari eyeballed the computer and the scanner, which was spitting out one of the documents. Then he grabbed the documents and made sure they were in order.

He looked at Tomlinson as he did so.

"You have a plan," he said.

"I do," she said.

"Care to share?" he asked.

"Not yet," she said. "But I do need you to do one thing."

His expression was impassive, which, she knew, was the look he got when he was bracing himself for something difficult.

"As soon as we know which courtroom we'll be in at ten, let the McHenrys know," she said.

"I thought you didn't want them there," he said.

She smiled. It was her feral courtroom smile.

"I do now," she said.

Tomlinson allowed herself one large mug of the very bad hotel coffee, and she ate a large breakfast of eggs, hashbrowns, and ham. She didn't sample the pastries that Kaitlyn had insisted on, and Tomlinson also stayed away from the specialty Starbucks coffees.

She took three bottles of water that had been left in the mostly bare kitchen and set them near her briefcase.

Then she sat in the very large living room, stared at the mountains, and worked on her argument. She always did that by hand. Her handwriting was deliberately atrocious so that her clients couldn't look over and argue with her talking points.

Besides, she preferred writing arguments by hand. They felt less ephemeral, and that technique meant that she often didn't have to look at the legal pad at all.

An hour before court, she took a wake-up shower to make sure she was completely alert, then put on her suit and some light make-up. She tucked her comfy shoes into her back and slipped on the Louboutins. She was going into the closed courthouse dressed to the nines, because she needed to look like the powerful attorney that she was.

She tasked Amari with meeting Brett McHenry in holding and making certain that he was ready for the arraignment. She had thought about assigning the job to David, the only white male on the team, but he didn't have the chops yet to handle regular assholes, let alone full-fledged psychopathic ones.

The team drove to the Regional Justice Center and parked in the nearly empty parking lot. Tomlinson had expected this part of downtown to be completely empty on Christmas morning, but it wasn't.

The chapel across the street from the parking lot had a series of weddings, one in their drive-through and another on the roof. A bride and groom were posing for professional pictures under the only tree near the parking lot's entrance, and another bride and groom were posing underneath the chapel's faux Las Vegas sign.

A line of people snaked around the Justice Center building, all waiting to get inside the Marriage License Bureau, which was, unfortunately, right next to the entrance for attorneys.

"Keep your heads down," she said. "There will be a lot of photos and social media postings."

She was using an excess of caution because very few people knew that her team was representing McHenry.

The morning still had its deep chill, and the sunlight wasn't doing much to dispel it. The light was thin at this time of year, almost anemic. Christmas carols, faint at first, reached Tomlinson's ears, and she worried that there would be carolers. Instead, it was a passel of bicyclists, with someone carrying an old-fashioned boom box on his shoulder as he pedaled.

The bicyclists covered one city block and then turned down the street between the wedding chapel and an over-sized condo complex. The music got loud, then faded as the cyclists hurried by.

"This town is strange," Kaitlyn said.

"You don't know the half of it," Tomlinson said.

She steered her team toward that entrance, which was between the Marriage License Bureau, the entrance for jurors, and the extra-large doors for the buses from the state prison. That part of the parking lot was empty as well.

County jail prisoners had a direct funnel into the court-house, which was fortunate. Amari had already taken a rideshare so that he would be in position when Brett McHenry arrived.

Tomlinson didn't seen the McHenry family. She had made it clear that they couldn't be anywhere near the defense team or the defense table once everyone was inside the courthouse.

She led her team up the stairs onto the broad plaza connecting the various entrances. No one from the Marriage License line seemed to notice her team at all. The couples and their families were all chatting with each other, posing for pictures near a gigantic red heart or underneath the red-and-green festooned ribbons around the bureau's windows.

A judicial clerk waited just inside the door, unlocking it as the team entered. The clerk was a heavyset woman with tired eyes, maybe fifty, maybe a little older. Clearly not someone who had children at home, but who might have had grandchildren to spend the day with.

"Thank you," Tomlinson said.

"Don't thank me," the clerk said. "And don't thank Judge Sanchez either. She doesn't want you to acknowledge how unusual this is, especially on the record."

"All right," Tomlinson said. She wondered what favors were pulled to get Sanchez here—or what skeletons were threatened with release from which closet.

It had been years since Tomlinson had been inside this building. It was as beautiful as she remembered. Even on a day like today, the three-story glass atrium was filled with sunlight. Nearby trees that made the entire interior seem like an outdoor plaza, and well-designed staircases to the upper floors.

A huge Christmas tree seemed dwarfed by the size of the indoor plaza. The tree had no decorations besides lights, and they weren't on, so it looked like a lost evergreen stationed in an unfamiliar land.

"Follow me to the courtroom," the clerk said, and led Tomlinson to the elevators. Her team trailed behind, subdued by the eeriness of being in a mostly closed courthouse on Christmas Day.

The courtrooms in this building weren't as grand as that entrance. They appeared to be an afterthought, almost too small to handle cases that might include a large interested gallery.

The courtroom that the clerk let them into was almost triangular. She flicked on the lights, making Tomlinson blink. There was a large overhead lightbox that was supposed to add space to the room, but only made the light more diffuse, as well as wall lamps that didn't add a lot of brightness to the room.

A jury box filled with upholstered blue chairs that were not so comfortable that the jury could easily fall asleep, but not so uncomfortable that they would hate sitting through a long trial. An industrial-strength gray carpet had been so recently cleaned that it still showed vacuum marks. All the wood in the room was a dark reddish that seemed more like it belonged in the 1970s than in a modern courtroom.

Her team slid into the benches behind the defense table. She set her briefcase underneath it, and her papers on top, along with her phone, in case she got a message from Amari.

The clerk vanished, leaving the team alone. No one spoke. The doors creaked behind them, then banged closed. Tomlinson didn't turn around. The door banged a second time, then a woman slid alone into the prosecutor's table.

She was small, silver-haired, and too thin with a mouth that pinched her narrow face even tighter. She didn't introduce herself. Instead, she nodded, her gaze flat, and then hauled her rather massive briefcase onto her chair, searching through an accordion file for something she seemed to have missed.

The door beside the judge's bench opened, and another woman entered. She had her dark hair piled on top of her head. She slipped into the chair for the court reporter and began to set up as well.

Then a different door opened, and Amari walked through, followed by two bailiffs escorting Brett McHenry. He wore a suit that was much too small for him. Judging by the suit's shiny silk and the size, the suit probably belonged to McHenry's father, because what 20-something brought a suit to his triumphal football weekend?

McHenry's piggy little eyes scanned the courtroom, then stopped moving when he saw something behind her. He smiled thinly, looking even younger than he was, confirming for her that his parents had entered at one point, just as she suspected.

Someone had let him wash his face, but his hands, still cuffed to his waist, were bruised around the knuckles. The edges of his fingernails were black.

Not that it meant anything. She already knew how to argue against any photos taken of that.

Ladies and gentlemen of the jury, the photos of Mr. McHenry's bruises at the time of his arrest simply mean that he had played a very rough and very successful four hours of football a few hours before.

He sank into a chair beside her, his chains clanking. He smelled faintly of sweat. Amari sat beside him on the far side.

Tomlinson turned slightly in her chair and leaned toward him. She knew that Amari had informed him of procedure, but she wanted to make sure of one thing.

"Everyone in this courtroom today is female," Tomlinson said. "You will treat us all with deference and respect, from the District Attorney to the judge. Do you understand?"

"Your boy told me that already," McHenry said.

It took all of her strength not to roll her eyes.

"Mr. Andersen is a capable attorney who is part of my team," Tomlinson said. "You will treat him with respect as well."

"Yes, ma'am," McHenry said, a tinge of resentment in his voice.

"And drop all of the attitude," Tomlinson said. "The more humble you seem, the better the chance of you waiting in jail for your trial."

"I can't—"

"Mr. McHenry," Tomlinson said. "I know you have an IQ. It's time for you to use it. You will utter exactly two words in this courtroom. Do you know what they are?"

"Not guilty," he said.

"That is correct. Now, sit back and practice looking deferential."

He glared at her, but he leaned back. The District

Attorney looked over at them from her table, as if she was taking McHenry's measure. Or maybe she was trying to figure out who Tomlinson was, exactly, to get a courtroom filled at 10 a.m. on Christmas morning.

"All rise for Judge Isabella Sanchez," the bailiff said.

Everyone stood. A tall woman in black judge's robes swept into the courtroom and ended up behind the bench. She surveyed everyone, her gaze finally landing on Tomlinson, as if measuring her as well.

It had begun.

The preliminaries took less than ten minutes. The judge read the charges, then asked McHenry to stand. He did so slowly, as if he had aged five decades while in prison.

"How do you plead?" she asked, her hooded gaze landing on him.

He cleared his throat, glanced at Tomlinson, who was surprised by his sudden nervousness, and then he said, "Not guilty, Your Honor."

Of course, speaking four words instead of the instructed two. Because that kid couldn't follow instructions from anyone. Or maybe from anyone who wasn't his father.

"Ms. Phan?" the judge said to the unlucky Christmas morning district attorney.

"We're asking for remand, your honor," Phan said. She had a flat, businesslike tone. "The defendant's crimes are heinous. We believe that it's only because the victim managed to get away that she's still alive."

McHenry grumbled, and Tomlinson hit him with her elbow, careful to make the move small and invisible to the judge.

"He's from out of state with no ties to the community," Phan said. "We believe it would better serve the interests of justice to keep him here in Nevada until trial."

"Ms. Tomlinson?" the judge asked.

"May we approach, Your Honor?" Tomlinson asked.

The judge frowned. Asking for a moment of the judge's time was unusual in an arraignment, which Tomlinson knew. She had no stake in the answer. She just wanted it on the record that she tried to keep her next remarks quiet.

"No," the judge said.

"Well, then," Tomlinson said, as if she actually were disappointed. "We have examined these charges, and they're based on illegally obtained evidence. The security videos in question were not obtained by the police or the district attorney's office. The videos were aired on television networks without my client's permission. His Name, Image, and Likeness are protected through legal relationships with his sports agency—"

"You can argue this in trial, Ms. Tomlinson," the judge said.

"I'm aware of that, Your Honor, but right now, my

client stands accused of crimes that have no evidentiary basis. We would prefer to have the charges dropped—"

"Of course you would," the judge said, "but that's not how things work in Nevada. Maybe in California."

"I've practiced in both locations, your honor," Tomlinson said. "We—"

"Your motion, if that's what that was, is denied," the judge said.

Tomlinson nodded. She had expected no less.

"We'll hear you on bail," the judge said, "and nothing more."

"My client has never been charged with a crime in any jurisdiction," Tomlinson said. She was choosing her words carefully because she did not want to commit to a boys-will-be-boys defense. "He is a known sports figure, especially after his performance at the Sin City College Football Bowl yesterday. His father is a well-known attorney. For those reasons, as well as the thinness of the district attorney's case, we ask that the defendant be released on his own recognizance, to return to Nevada for any scheduled trial."

The judge studied Tomlinson for a moment, tilting her head slightly, knowing what Tomlinson had just done. Then the judge turned her attention to the district attorney.

"Ms. Phan, is this correct? Do you have the security video?"

"We have subpoenaed it, Your Honor."

The judge let out a gusty sigh. "So that is a no. What do you have?"

"Right now, we have the victim's statement to the police, statements from bystanders—"

"Any in that elevator?" the judge asked.

"It was just the defendant and the victim in the elevator, Your Honor," the district attorney said.

"So that's a no as well," the judge said.

"And we have videos and photos from various witnesses…"

"Voluntarily given?" the judge asked.

"Um, no, Your Honor," Phan said. "We've subpoenaed those as well. We will have them shortly."

"Shortly does us no good right now," the judge said. She looked like she had swallowed something bad. Maybe she had. The fact that this arraignment had been scheduled on Christmas had interfered with the DA's office's evidence collection.

To her credit, the judge did not look at Tomlinson, whose request made this moment possible. Instead, the judge folded her hands and leaned forward.

"Right now, we have a possible domestic violence case, which I will have to treat like all other domestic violence cases. This case is unusual in that we have a well-known defendant from out of state, but that's the only factor I can consider at the moment. So, I will set bail at half a million dollars—"

"Your Honor!" Phan said.

"Which is high enough considering the fact that the defendant does not live in Nevada." The judge scanned the courtroom. "Is the defendant's father here?"

Tomlinson turned slightly and saw the older McHenry. He looked very serious—probably his courtroom face. His wife sat next to him, her hands clutched over the front of her gaudy Alexander McQueen blazer.

"Yes, Your Honor," Tomlinson said.

"Sir, will you step forward?" the judge asked.

The younger McHenry turned and watched his father approach the small gate that separated the audience gallery from the actual court itself. The older McHenry's hand waivered at the small gate door, but then he decided not to open it.

It was a good call. He seemed less arrogant that way.

"Is it true, sir," the judge said, "that you are an officer of the court?"

"Yes, your honor," he said. "I am a lawyer—"

The judge waved her hand, shutting him up. "You will give my clerk all the pertinent information regarding your law license, and we will file it with the particulars of this case. If your son does not arrive at the appointed meetings and times, we will contact you. If you facilitate his inability to come to court, we will report you to your local bar. Is that clear?"

"Yes, Your Honor," McHenry said.

"You may sit down now," the judge said.

He returned to his seat. Tomlinson found herself wishing that his son was as cooperative.

"Bail is set," the judge said. "We shall work now on trial dates." And she beckoned her clerk over.

Tomlinson was not going to mention any of her other cases. She would let the DA and the judge set the timetable, and she was going to hope that the dates would conflict with something else she already had scheduled.

She was going to do whatever it took to step away from this case.

The younger McHenry had his head down to hide a smile. The small celebration was inappropriate. She knew that his parents probably were not celebrating since they knew this ordeal had just begun.

Still, Tomlinson dutifully pulled out her paper calendar and worked with the judge, scheduling a trial that she never meant to attend.

Tomlinson took her time packing her briefcase. The bailiff took the younger McHenry back to process him and give him the rest of his belongings.

Tomlinson got the sense that no one in the local justice system thought McHenry would be released this morning. She sent Amari with them to make sure that nothing went wrong.

The rest of her team had already left the courtroom.

She slung her bag over her shoulder and gripped the handle on her case as she turned around.

The older McHenry and his wife were heading out the door. They took the stairs down, which somehow surprised Tomlinson. She would have expected them to eschew exercise. But then, given the look of Mrs. McHenry's legs, maybe exercise was all they had in common.

Tomlinson followed them down the stairs. She wanted to talk with the older McHenry, but not in the courtroom itself.

"Sir," she said, as they reached the atrium. "A word?"

He patted his wife's shoulder and walked closer to the gigantic Christmas tree. Tomlinson joined him.

"Good work in there," he said before she had a chance to speak. "I would rather have him leave without charges, but this is second best."

She bristled internally. This was the best anyone could have done.

"We're heading to put up the bail right now. I have the card of a recommended bondsman." He thrust it at her. She saw the logo and nodded.

"They're not far from here," she said. "You can walk."

He nodded and started to walk away. Apparently, the arrogant asshole thought that she had wanted his compliments.

"Before you leave, sir," she said, "I've been thinking about this case."

He waited, as if she was on the verge of wasting his time.

"I think you're right. You should handle the case. I think you need a different Nevada attorney at your side."

He gave her a tiny victorious smile, rather like his son's celebration smile in the courtroom.

"That attorney needs to be a white male," she said, "because your son has obvious problems with women and people of color."

The older McHenry's face flushed. "My son is no more a bigot than I am."

"Then I'm very sorry for you, sir," Tomlinson said. She had always hated that sentence.

His flush grew deeper.

"I would recommend that your son gets therapy and some sensitivity training in the next several months. I have no idea how he's survived on football teams. I suspect everyone tolerates him because he's so good. But he won't be on a team now. He'll be in a courtroom in one of the most diverse states in the country. His attitudes might get him convicted."

"With a lesser lawyer," the older McHenry said viciously, "he might. But you're right. I'll handle the case going forward."

She had provoked the barb, so it didn't bother her. "I'll make sure you have the paperwork to terminate me from this case. We will also share our notes and filings and what we have found so far. Contact my office, and we'll get this underway after the holidays."

Then she pivoted without saying goodbye and walked to her team. They had clustered near one of the regular trees. They looked small and tired in the large room.

The older McHenry stood for a moment near the Christmas tree, then squared his shoulders and returned to his wife. He was smart enough to suspect he had just been played, although he might not have known how thoroughly.

He put his hand on his wife's back and led her out of the door that was usually used for jurors. They were on their way to pay bail.

Tomlinson let out a sigh. She and the rest of the team would wait for Amari near the car, but she wanted to give the McHenrys a few moments to get ahead of them.

"So, what, you resigned?" David asked.

She looked at him. "You could hear that?"

"No," he said. "But you approached him. I couldn't think of any other reason you'd voluntarily talk with him."

"Maybe tell him to keep his son under control until trial." Kaitlyn's voice held barely contained fury. She was clutching her hands into fists. "You know he'll just attack someone in podunk's ville while he's under what passes for house arrest."

"After today, he won't be our concern anymore, Kaitlyn." Tomlinson kept her voice gentle.

"No, he'll just go back to being a serial attacker, and no

one will hold him to account for his behavior here." Kaitlyn's face had gone red as well.

Tomlinson let out a small laugh. "Well, you never do know how a trial by jury will go. What we do know is that this young man and his father will not plead the case out."

"They could. You showed them how to torpedo the evidence," Kaitlyn said.

Kaitlyn's emotions were getting in the way of her brilliant legal mind. But Tomlinson didn't say that.

"Did I?" Tomlinson asked.

Kaitlyn hesitated, suddenly realizing that she had missed something important.

"The videos—all of them—will be subpoenaed within the next few days. There will be testimony from the posse as they realize they're being hung out to dry while their ringleader goes home. By the way, did anyone figure out why they were beating that kid?"

"He was a star player for one of the other regional teams who didn't make the playoffs," David said. "I guess he and his girlfriend came here to cheer the locals on."

"He was a rival," Nita added. "And McHenry was drunk. I think the attack on Keesha wasn't on her at all, but to show the rival that McHenry had the bigger dick."

Tomlinson shuddered. Somehow, all of that made it worse.

She looked at Kaitlyn. "I told Mr. McHenry that he should handle the case, and he should have a white male lawyer at his side."

"On a sexual *assault* case?" Kaitlyn said. "That's no longer standard procedure—Oh." And then she smiled. "He's going to do that, isn't he?"

Tomlinson nodded. "I did recommend that his son get therapy and sensitivity training. That will be in the documents we send over to them. Of course, it will go unheeded, since Mr. McHenry told me that his son is no more bigoted than he is."

A laugh sounded behind her. She turned. Amari was standing there, paperwork in hand.

"If the McHenrys are the standard for no bigotry, then we're all in more trouble than I thought," Amari said.

"Is the kid ready to go once they pay bail?" Tomlinson asked.

"Yeah," Amari said. "Not that he's grateful or even kind. He wanted to know how we can quash everything to make sure there won't be coverage of this around the draft."

"Hmm." Tomlinson permitted herself a tiny smile. "Well, we're done quashing things."

Nita nodded, then grabbed her phone and walked toward the doors.

"We will send any documents we have, but not much more. I'll write a cover letter acknowledging my upcoming termination." Tomlinson paused for one delicious moment. "The documents we send, by the way, will only be what we have from here in Las Vegas. Any work that's been done in Los Angeles by our various teams isn't yet part of our files and won't be until I'm off this case. Is that clear?"

There was silence for a moment, then Kaitlyn barked a laugh. "You're not going to give them any real help, are you?"

Tomlinson smiled at her. "I did today. That's about all I can stomach."

"I would be happier if he went to jail for a long time," Kaitlyn said.

"Trust the system," Tomlinson said.

"I don't, really," Kaitlyn said. "There's too many ifs. What if the jury likes him? What if—"

"The ifs are always with us," Tomlinson said. "We've chosen the defense side of the adversarial relationship. That means we deal with foul people a lot. There are other places in the law that can be tweaked to help victims. This is not one of them."

She would probably pull Kaitlyn aside early in the new year and recommend that she move to some form of victim's advocacy. Defense wasn't going to be her strength. She had too much empathy.

Tomlinson walked toward the door, trusting her team to follow. With high-end clients, empathy was a detriment to doing her job well. Maybe if she was a public defender, empathy might help her.

But here? She dealt with scum most of the time. Rich scum. Scum who presented her with legal challenges that kept her prodigious brain busy, especially since she always wanted to win, and win big.

This morning was a win in court, on the merits. Not

even getting a hearing this morning was bending the rules. She would have argued, as an outsider, against Nevada's penchant for blowing off arraignments during holidays.

But she hadn't had to haul out that card. She had done what she needed to do and said what she needed to say to Mr. We're-Not-A-Family-Of-Bigoted-Assholes.

That was a win enough for her.

But today was also a warning. That moment when she saw her own daughter's face instead of Keesha's might have been an internal shot across the bow. Tomlinson might not be able to do this kind of work much longer, not and maintain the respect of her children.

That was, though, a problem for another day. This day's problem now was checking out of their suite, and heading to the jet. It wasn't even noon yet.

She would call her husband and tell him she would be home in time for their big Christmas dinner. Then she would sleep on the jet, knowing she had done the best she could with the tools she'd been handed, knowing that for now, anyway, she remained in the eyes of her staff and colleagues, Catherine the Great.

TSLAND
TREASURE
MGM
THE CITY OF
ENTERTAINMENT
LUXOR
EXCALIBUR

BUT WAIT, THERE'S MORE!

Want more masterful mysteries?

Go to wmgbooks.com!

Sign up for the Kristine Kathryn Rusch newsletter, and keep up with the latest news, releases and so much more— even the occasional giveaway.

To sign up go to kriswrites.com

Get the latest news and releases from all of WMG's authors and lines, including Kristine Grayson, Kris Nelscott, *Pulphouse Magazine*, and so much more…

To sign up, **go to wmgbooks.com.**

ABOUT THE AUTHOR
KRISTINE KATHRYN RUSCH

Kristine Kathryn Rusch sold more than 35 million books worldwide. She publishes bestselling science fiction and fantasy, award-winning mysteries, acclaimed mainstream fiction, controversial nonfiction, and the occasional romance.

Her novels made bestseller lists around the world and her short fiction appeared in more than twenty best-of-the-year collections. She won more than twenty-five awards for her fiction, including the Hugo, *Le Prix Imaginales*, the *Asimov's* Readers Choice award, and the *Ellery Queen Mystery Magazine* Readers Choice Award.

To find out more about her work, go to her website, kriswrites.com

facebook.com/kristinekathrynruschwriter

patreon.com/kristinekathrynrusch

bookbub.com/authors/kristine-kathryn-rusch

TREASURE ISLAND
MGM
THE CITY OF ENTERTAINMENT
LUXOR
EXCALIBUR